W9-CPQ-657

FEATHER FIN

Written By:
STEPHEN COSGROVE

Illustrated By
ROBIN JAMES

GROLIER ENTERPRISES INC.
Danbury, Connecticut

A Serendipity™ Book

Dedicated to Todd Hiatt and his Peacock Eel. May they both live forever in a land of feathers, fins, and ferns.

The moon of many moods lighted the night sky as it pulled and pushed the waters of the ocean, creating swells that gently washed against the shore. The moonlight skipped across the waves, casting its glow and shadows far out to sea.

Beneath the surface of waves the movement of the water was stilled. The sights of light and bright were subdued in the crystal blue waters that swirled in and around the sea-water ferns.

All the fish of the sea, colored yellow to blue, red to green, swam about the pillars of coral, swirling around the serene water.

Amidst all the fish of the sea lived beautiful but strange little creatures called Peacock Eels. Their fins, like feathers, swished gently back and forth as they swam effortlessly in the tides and eddies of the atoll. The older eels searched about the bottom for tidbits and morsels to eat while the young played in and about the under-water castles of coral and sand.

As the creatures moved about in poetic ease, one little eel, more brightly colored than all the rest stayed still within the waters and looked up. He watched as the movement of the waves high above caused the light to shift and dance on the water like a rainbow of color.

He was born in an ivory-colored egg and all the other fish called him Feather-Fin.

Feather Fin spent all of his days looking for beautiful, colorful things. He floated for hours and hours, watching the light playing upon the facets of diamond coral. The other eels would swim around him, begging him to play. They would surround him as he lay motionless in the water, blowing bubbles at him or flipping their tails; but no matter—he just wouldn't budge.

The other eels would soon tire of their games and swim away, leaving Feather Fin to gaze at the beauty around him. When he was sure that he was all alone he would turn his eyes up to the surface of the sea. For, you see, Feather Fin had only one dream in the whole world—and that was to visit the mysterious land of High Above.

Once he had asked his mother-eel about the beautiful colors that played upon the surface. "It would be such fun to go there and see all there is to see," he said in wide-eyed wonder.

"Never! Never!" his mother bubbled back at him. "You must never go to the land of High Above. It's not made for fish like you or me."

"Oh, pooh and seaweed!" he burbled as he swam away. "What do mothers know? Someday I will go there and see what I must see."

Then, late one day as the darkness of the night curled in with the afternoon tide, Feather Fin slipped away to hide. He swam and swam away from his home to the higher corals and softer sands of the shallows of the sea.

In a small niche he hid and watched as the other eels and fish swam safely for their caves to sleep away the period of darkness.

He waited and when the nighttime was almost gone, just before the first light of dawn, he began swimming higher and higher. The silvery light of High Above beckoned to him as he fluttered his feathery fins, struggling to climb up to the surface.

The waves broke about him as Feather Fin popped to the surface of the sea. There before him he saw, for the first time, the golden sands of a beach.

Then, just as he sighed in wonder at it all, a wave larger than all the rest picked him up like a leaf and gently washed him onto the shore.

Feather Fin was amazed at all the beauty around him. There were gently waving palm trees softly sighing in the off-shore breeze, and at the edge of the sand, brightly colored flowers in all the colors of the rainbow. Of course, he had never before heard the rustling of the wind, nor the bell-like crashing of waves on the shore, and the sound was like music to his ears.

Then, as he breathed deeply through his gills, he suddenly tasted what was to him the terrible unbreathable air of High Above. Feather Fin gasped and realized, too late, that his mother was right, that this place was not for fish to see. He struggled and flipped and flopped, trying to get back into the water, but to no avail.

There he lay on the sand, panting, wishing that he had never left the safety of the sea.

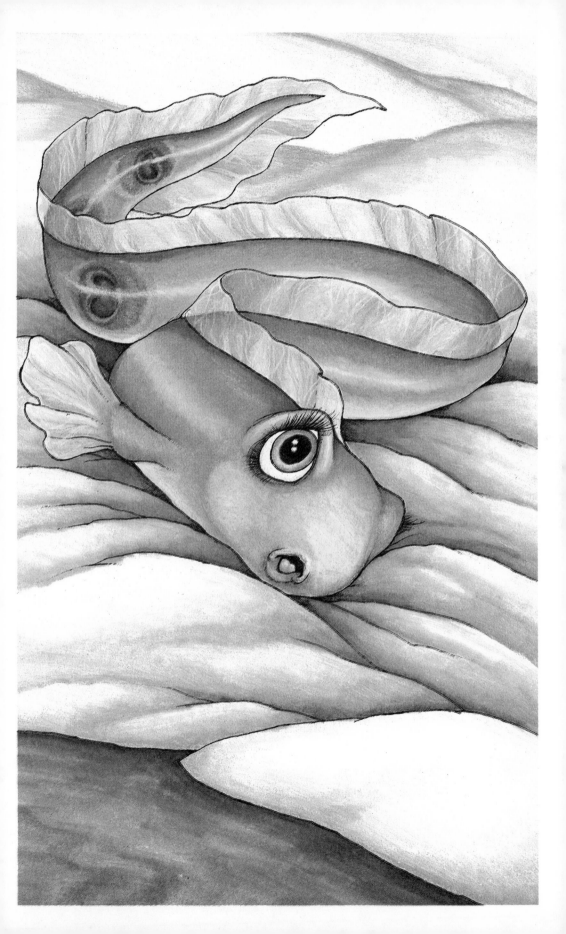

Just as Feather Fin thought that all was lost, the last, large wave of an ebbing tide gently lapped about him and he quickly slipped back into the water. He swam around and around, washing all the sandy traces of High Above from his fins. Satisfied that he was clean at last, Feather Fin swam back to his home in the deep.

From that day on and forever more, the little Peacock Eel stayed and played with the other fish at the bottom of the sea. He played bubble-up and bubble-down and never once did he dream of the land of High Above.

IF YOU'RE LOOKING
FOR ADVENTURE
AND YOUR PARENTS
HAVE TOLD YOU, "NO!"
DREAM OF AN EEL
CALLED FEATHER FIN
AND ALL THE THINGS
HE CAME TO KNOW